A BROKEN
GIRL'S JOURNEY 2

NATIONAL BEST SELLING AUTHOR
NIKI JILVONTAE

A Broken Girl's Journey 2
-Written By-
Niki Jilvontae

Copyright © 2021 by Niki Jilvontae
Facebook: Niki Jilvontae
Instagram: NikiJilvontae

This novel is a work of fiction. Any resemblances to actual events, real people, living or dead, organizations, establishments or locales are products of the author's imagination. Other names, characters, places, and incidents are used fictitiously.

Cover Design: Tina Louise
Editor: Tamyra L. Griffin

Dedication

I dedicate this book to the Me of the past! To the broken girl who had just began the hardest parts of her journey when this book was originally published in 2014!

**2021 Niki Jilvontae to 2014 Niki: "Congratulations... I'm so proud of you! Look at what you accomplished in 7 years! 70 Books!! See what happens when You believe in YOU!! I love you and don't forget that!!

Acknowledgements

First, I have to thank the Most High for this incredible gift! Àse! I'd also like to thank my children author Ny'Cole & King for always encouraging and inspiring me. To my bestie and beta reader, Ryan Smothers, thank you for being my sounding board and shoulder to lean on. To my divas Linette King & Tamyra Griffin, thank you both for simply being you! Real ain't and easy to come by so I value you just like I do my bestie Carmel Fason, my Tweety. Thank you for never folding on me in over 20 years of friendship. And to my readers like Ciera Lawrence, Tonya Russell, MyRe Child, Amanda Conners, Tru Diavolo, Charlene Atchison, and Shamone Shariff just to name a few! Thank you all for loving me and allowing me to love on you too through my words. To the rest of readers and supporters Love and Light along with a million thank you's to you too! Y'all just don't know how much the love means to me. I am forever grateful! Love and Light to you all! Namaste

Synopsis

After having her life turned upside down and her heart broken countless times, Lakea Johnson awakes from a coma and tries to begin picking up the pieces of her shattered world without her true love. Now a young woman, Lakea is still badly broken from the struggles of growing up in the violent streets of Memphis and she begins a downward spiral of drugs, violence, stripping, and volatile relationships. Soon Lakea realizes that her journey will be a long road paved in her blood and tears as she endures all the pain the world throws at her. Depression envelopes her and she feels all hope is gone until she finds light in the darkness, refuge from her pain. She finally starts to feel complete.... but will her happiness last? Or is her happiness the calm before the storm?

Table of Contents

Chapter 1

A loud bang from the killer's 9MM was the last sound Lakea heard before everything went black. Jeremy's face, his words, and that look of fear in his eyes kept playing over and over again in her mind. She felt herself floating somewhere far away from Frayser, far away from Memphis, far away from this world for that matter. She felt so pure, so innocent. All the burdens of her life seemed to have been lifted off of her shoulders. She felt complete for the first time in a long time, totally at peace, except there was nothing but darkness all around her; nothing but darkness and silence. Just then Lakea heard a voice.

"I love you my princess. I have missed you so much, but you have to go back.", the voice said.

Lakea looked around confused. She knew that voice, but it couldn't be.

"Lady Bug you have to go back because it's not your time. You have so much to live for. Go back and live your life. Be happy and forgive your mama. She has some hurtful things to tell you, but you still must forgive her.", the voice said.

Lakea reached out into the darkness. She knew that voice was her daddy's.

"Daddy is that you?" Lakea asked frantically.

"Daddy please come to me. Daddy I don't want to go back, and I don't want to forgive mama; I want to stay with you." Lakea said trying to peer through the darkness.

"You can't baby, and you have to forgive her even after she tells you what she has to say. Know that she loves you so much and so do I. Never forget that Lady Bug", Marvin, Lakea's dad, said as his voice began to trail off.

"Daddy, what does she have to tell me and why can't I stay?!" Lakea yelled, but her daddy was gone.

She was alone again in the darkness. Just then through the darkness Lakea saw a ray of light and Jeremy appeared. He was beautiful and glowing. As clear as day he stood before her eyes. Lakea reached her arms out to hold him, and to her surprise he was still there. She could feel his smooth, chocolate skin under her fingertips. Jeremy pulled her into the light, and she stared into his beautiful gray eyes. They floated there in the ray of light for a while, saying nothing, just holding each other. Then Jeremy spoke.

"Baby, I love you, but you have to go back."

Lakea shook her head no. She didn't want to go back. She wanted to stay with Jeremy and be in his arms forever.

"Noooo, I don't want to go back; I want to stay with you and my daddy." Lakea said, holding Jeremy close to her and laying her head on his chest.

She could smell his cologne. He stroked her hair and inhaled her scent like he always did. Then he slowly lifted her head and spoke.

"Baby, you have to go, it's not your time." Jeremy said with tears in his eyes.

"I don't care if it's my time or not, I want to be with you. I have nothing to live for." Lakea said as Jeremy gently caressed her cheek.

"Yes, you do. You have Quan who needs you and RayRay needs you too,"

Lakea shook her head no as her tears began to flow again.

"No, they took Ray-Ray away from me too, and soon Quan will be gone off doing his own thang too and I will be all alone. I need to be with you!" Lakea whined.

"No Ray-Ray is still with you baby, and he will need you. Y'all will need each other, but I know someone else who will need you more", Jeremy said wiping the tears from Lakea's eyes.

"Who?" Lakea asked.

She was certain that he meant her mama, but what he said next changed everything.

"You have to go back for our child", Jeremy said rubbing Lakea's stomach, then bending down to kiss it.

By then the tears had begun to flow down his face and Lakea gasped for air. She couldn't believe what she was hearing. Lakea wiped away Jeremy's tears and pulled him close to her. She loved him so much and it was apparent that he loved her just as much as she loved him, and now she would have their child to love. Suddenly the sound of trumpets startled Lakea and Jeremy.

"I have to go." Jeremy said with tears still streaming down his face.

"And so, do you. Live life to its fullest baby; never take one second for granted. And tell my son that I loved him with all of me. Baby please makeup with your mama too." Jeremy pleaded.

Lakea turned her head and began to protest. She couldn't understand why everyone wanted her to forgive her mama. She couldn't see then how that resentment was hurting her. Jeremy grabbed Lakea's chin and turned her face back to him.

"Baby our child deserves a mother with a loving heart. Besides, she doesn't deserve your hate. I bet if you talk to her you may find out y'all have more in common and you may just begin to understand why she did all she has done; either way baby you have to let it go!" Jeremy pleaded with tears rolling down his face.

Tears were falling from Lakea's eyes too. She felt Jeremy's love and she knew that he and her father were right. She had to find a way to forgive her mama, not only for herself, but for the sake of her child too.

"Okay baby." Lakea whispered into his ear. "But I still don't want to live without you", Lakea pleaded.

"You won't be without me, ever!" Jeremy said. "I will never leave you. I will always be right here." Jeremy said touching his hand to Lakea's heart.

Just then Lakea felt relief she had never felt before. She felt a love greater than she had ever imagined. Her broken heart was starting to mend. Jeremy kissed her slowly and deeply. Lakea could feel his soul as they kissed passionately while looking into each other's eyes. Their whole life together flashed before her eyes in that instant and she knew then that Jeremy's flesh was gone forever. Suddenly the light began to disappear, and Jeremy began to back away from her into the darkness.

"Don't forget I will never stop loving you." Jeremy said as he disappeared into the darkness, leaving Lakea crying and screaming his name.

He was gone and she was alone again, floating in the darkness. Just then she heard Quan's voice.

Chapter 2

"She been in a coma forever, she ain't gone never come back to us." Quan whimpered.

Lakea tried hard to open her eyes but they felt glued shut. She tried again and her eye lids fluttered.

"Wait, she's waking up!" Quan yelled as Lakea opened up her beautiful hazel eyes.

She was out of the darkness. She was alive! Lakea stared up into the bright lights over her hospital bed. She was so confused. Had it all been a dream? Did she really hear her father talking to her? Did she really see Jeremy? Suddenly as she stared up at the ceiling and her eyes moved frantically back and forth before her brother Quan's face came into focus. There he stood as handsome as ever with a worried look on his face and tears falling from his eyes. Lakea tried to turn her head but it felt heavy and stuck to the bed.

"Lakea!" Quan said crying as he laid his head on his big sister's chest.

Lakea moved her arm and rubbed her brother's head as he embraced her.

"She woke y'all!" Quan yelled running to the door as Anterrius, Anthony, MJ, Mesha, and Aunt Violet came rushing into the room.

Lakea stared up into their loving faces going around the room. Then she noticed her standing in the back with her head down, it was her mama Felicia. Standing next to

Felicia was a man Lakea recognized as her uncle Jacob, her daddy's best friend from childhood. He was tall and handsome with skin the same color as Lakea's and hazel, almond shaped eyes just like hers. He was Lakea's favorite uncle because he always played with her and brought her the best gifts when he came from Atlanta to visit. He called her his twin, his chocolate chip. Lakea looked back at Felicia and saw that tears were running down her cheeks and she was praying.

"Mama", Lakea said weakly.

Everyone looked amazed as they cleared a path for Felicia so that she could stand right by Lakea. Lakea remembered how Jeremy and her father told her she had to let it go. She knew that it was necessary, and she was willing to give it a try.

"I'm sorry, baby. I'm so, so very sorry for everything!" Felicia cried as she kissed and held Lakea's hand. "I love you baby, please forgive me!" Felicia begged.

Tears started to fall from Lakea's eyes. She loved her mama - and even though she had hurt her so much in her life, Lakea hated to see her mama in pain. Lakea tried to turn her head again but she still couldn't.

"Why can't I turn my head mama?" Lakea asked weakly.

Just then a tall, handsome Caucasian doctor and two nurses walked in.

"Oh, I see our patient is finally awake." the doctor said, smiling at Lakea as he checked her vitals, and the nurses went about fixing medications and preparing for her sponge bath.

"How nice of you to join us young lady after 2 and a half months." the doctor said with a chuckle and Lakea's heart dropped.

Lakea couldn't believe it. She had been in a coma for two and a half months.

"What happened to me?" She whispered.

The room had begun to spin, and she felt like she was falling.

"Well sweetie…" The doctor said looking into Lakea's eyes with a light. "You were shot two times, once in your head and once in the abdomen. The bullet that entered your head right above your temple came out behind your ear, missing your skull. That's why you cannot move your head." the doctor said taking the brace off of her head.

"We had to keep it stabilized until you were awake, and we knew the extent of your injuries. There wasn't much structural damage done, but there was some neurological damage that caused your coma, and which may require physical therapy to ensure full mobility of your limbs,"

Just then Lakea remembered what Jeremy had said.

"You have to go back for our child!"

She was pregnant.

'Oh my!' Lakea thought.

"Didn't he just say I was shot in the stomach?" Lakea began to panic.

She couldn't lose her baby too, her only piece of Jeremy.

"What about my baby?" Lakea asked frantically.

Everyone in the room looked confused and amazed.

"How does she know that she is pregnant?" Mesha asked Quan with a bewildered look on her face.

Lakea heard Mesha's question, so she turned her head slowly to look at Mesha and reply.

"Jeremy told me." Lakea said in a matter-of-fact tone.

Everyone looked at each other then back at Lakea with sympathy in their eyes.

"Your baby is okay", Aunt Violet said.

Just then Lakea reached down and touched her stomach. Then she felt it...LIFE! Her stomach was round and starting to protrude. She could feel her baby growing inside of her. Then with tears rolling down her face Felicia spoke to her daughter.

"Baby, Jeremy didn't make it."

Those words hurt Lakea to her core, but she already knew it. Jeremy had already given her the strength she needed to get through it. She had her baby, and she was going to be the best mama she could be.

"I know.", Lakea said as the tears fell from her eyes. Felicia and Violet hugged her.

Lakea could feel her mama's love for the first time in a long time. Just then the hospital door swung open and Lakea could hear the click of crutches hit the linoleum floor. She looked at Quan's face as he stared towards the door then looked back at her smiling. She wanted to know who it was he was smiling about. Lakea tried to stretch her neck to see around Mesha, but she couldn't. Mesha stepped to the side and Lakea could see who had just entered her room. Standing before her, walking on crutches due to the stab wound that was close to his spine was Ray-Ray, her big brother. Lakea gasped loudly and then burst into tears. Her brother was alive and looked just like she remembered except for visible scares on his face and the crutches he had to use now to get around. Ray-Ray got to his sister as fast as he could and began to hug and plant kisses all over her face and cheeks. Lakea cried uncontrollably, thanking the Lord for bringing her brother through. Ray-Ray cried too as he held his sister tight and stroked her hair.

"I love you lil sis - and I told you I would never leave you." Ray-Ray whispered into Lakea's ear as she sobbed and held on to him.

"Can I have a few minutes alone with my sister please?" Ray-Ray asked, wiping the snot and tears from his face.

Everyone hugged and kissed Lakea before they left the room. Jacob waited behind and slowly made his way to Lakea's bed.

"Hey chocolate chip." Jacob said handing her a dozen of pink roses, her favorite.

"I just wanted to tell you how much I love you, and I would love to talk to you once you heal and get settled."

"Okay Uncle Jacob - and love you too." Lakea said, staring up at him as he kissed her forehead and stared down at her battered body.

He had a faraway look in his eyes. Lakea wondered what he wanted to talk about. Once Jacob left the room Ray-Ray sat on the bed beside her, looking into her eyes while rubbing her stomach.

"Lil sis, I'm sorry about Jeremy." Ray-Ray said as Lakea sobbed. "But you gotta know that maine loved you with all of his heart."

Lakea shook her head yes, indicating she knew how much Jeremy loved her.

"I saw Jeremy the day I got fucked up and he gave me some stuff to give to you." Ray-Ray said as he took a small pink box and a long pink box out of his pocket.

"It was like he knew something was going to happen to him and he wanted to make sure that you would be alright." Ray Ray said staring at the boxes in his hand.

Lakea began to cry a little harder thinking about how strong Jeremy's love was for her, and how she may never find another man to ever love and care about her as much as he did.

Ray-Ray opened the long pink box he held in his hand and showed Lakea its contents. Inside was a key ring with a picture of them in high school attached to it. There were also two keys on the key ring inside the box along with a beautiful platinum chain with a heart shaped locket on it. Lakea wept and thought of her one true love as her brother unhooked the clasp and put the locket around her neck.

Lakea touched the locket with her fingertips then she pulled the long chain up to her face and opened the locket to see pictures of herself and Jeremy inside. Lakea kissed Jeremy's picture then closed the locket and laid it over top of her heart while staring at her brother.

Ray-Ray looked at Lakea with sympathy, love, and a familiar heavy heart. He had lost a love too. Even though his girlfriend had set him up to be jumped, she was still the mother of his child, and now she was dead; killed by his own little brother, so he knew the pain that his little sister was now feeling oh too well.

"These keys are to your new truck and your house. Jeremy did it all himself. He wanted to make sure you had a chance at a normal life."

Lakea couldn't believe how much Jeremy had actually loved her. He thought of her in his last moments of life. His last words had been, "I love you."

Lakea could still hear those words and see the look in Jeremy's eyes. She rubbed her stomach and felt Jeremy's love. It was as if he had his strong hands on her stomach and he was kissing their baby. He said that he would never leave her, and Lakea believed him. She could feel Jeremy still with her.

"When you get out of here, I will take you to your truck and your house. He got you a Ford Freestyle, and your house is in a very nice neighborhood in Cordova."

Lakea took the keys and held them close to her heart.

"What was in the other box?" Lakea asked with a raspy voice.

Her throat hurt from all of the crying she had been doing, it made it hard for her to talk.

"Oh, this box was found on the ground next to his bod..." Ray-Ray said in a sad voice, cutting off the word as he opened the box revealing a Mosaica 2ct. TW diamond engagement ring in 14K gold.

Ray-Ray slipped the ring on to his sister's ring finger as she began to cry hysterically again. It would be years before she took that ring off.

"He was going to marry me." Lakea said sobbing. "That's why he stopped at the door. He was going to propose to me, but..." Lakea said as her body began to shake.

"But they came and took him from me forever!" Lakea cried as her brother held her and cried with her.

Just then Ray-Ray closed his eyes while holding his sister and began to sing the lyrics to the song she wrote and sang to him when he was in the hospital. Her song had helped him to hold on and fight through one of the most difficult times in his life, so now he was going to use her words to help her get through this tragedy. Ray-Ray sang the lyrics of Lakea's song with so much love and passion it made her stop crying and look up at his face.

"Love hard, be inspired, and Smile often...always reaching higher. You gotta hold on...because love is worth it!" Ray-Ray sang looking into his sister's eyes as he held her.

Lakea let her heavy eyelids close and drifted off, dreaming about the baby growing inside of her and her one true love.

Chapter 3

Lakea had to stay in the hospital the next few weeks until her doctor was confident she would be able to carry her baby without difficulty. All of her physical wounds had healed quickly, but her emotional scars were deep. Lakea would go from happy to sad in seconds. She could not control her emotions. She was trying so hard to be strong that it was tearing her apart. However, her family was right there to support her.

Everyone was so worried about her. Ray-Ray and Quan were right there every second helping her. They even helped her to the bathroom, even though it was less than six feet away. What they didn't know and what Lakea didn't even know herself was that she was much stronger than she ever knew - and with good reason. Now she had a real purpose in life; a real reason to not just exist and inflict pain on others, but to be someone. Lakea's purpose in life now was to be a mother, and she was going to be the best mother that she could be.

Felicia came by a lot while Lakea was in the hospital recovering. She and her mother were slowly getting their relationship to a good place. On the day before Lakea was to be released from the hospital Felicia and a tall, dark hair white woman with glasses entered her room. Lakea looked up confused. She wondered what was going on and why Felicia had brought the woman there to see her.

'She better not be trying to take my baby.' Lakea thought as they approached her bed.

"Hey baby." Felicia said kissing Lakea on the head.

Lakea managed a weak smile, but she kept her eyes on the woman.

"Hi Lakea, my name is Dr. Andrea Roth, and I am a licensed psychiatrist. I was wondering would you like to talk to me?"

Lakea rolled her eyes.

"I may be able to help you with some of those thoughts and feelings you are having about being pregnant. You're three months now, right?" Dr. Roth asked sitting down in the chair next to Lakea's bed.

Lakea shook her head yes and stared out of the window. She didn't want to talk to Dr. Roth. She didn't want to tell anyone about how much she was hurting and how badly she didn't want to live without Jeremy had it not been for her baby. However, Lakea did want to give healing a chance. She had promised so many people that she would try to get better and not resist help, so that is what she was going to do despite how much she just wanted to curl up in a ball and die. Lakea knew that she had to get herself together for her baby's sake. She turned to face the doctor with the most pained and hurt look on her face.

"Can you help me to deal with Jeremy's death?" Lakea asked with a tear rolling down her cheek.

"Yes, I can." Dr. Roth said smiling warmly at Lakea.

"Can you help me to build a better relationship with my mama, and her with my brothers too?" Lakea asked, weeping as Felicia grabbed her and wiped away her tears.

"Yes, I definitely can help with that too. You are going to be just fine Lakea, I promise you that. You are a very strong young woman, and you will get through this all. You just have to trust me and let the therapy work." Dr. Roth said, rubbing Lakea's hand.

Lakea hoped that she was right, and she hoped that she didn't have to be completely broken again in order for her to finally become complete. Lakea wasn't sure if her broken heart could take anymore tragedy, and she didn't want to find out.

Dr. Roth spoke with Lakea and Felicia for a while longer, going over the therapy plan. Lakea would begin individual therapy once a week, and group therapy three times a week. Then after a month or so they would start family counseling with her and Felicia, and then later add the boys in. As she sat there listening to Dr. Roth talk, Lakea thought back to when they all had to see a psychiatrist after their father died. That therapy wasn't very effective because none of them really wanted to be there, and Felicia did not see the importance. Instead, they just let all of their emotions, all of the pain, hurt and loss fester and turn into destructive attitudes and behaviors.

"Maybe it will work this time?" Lakea said out loud.

"It will baby, I promise!" Felicia said hugging Lakea before she left the room to walk Dr. Roth out.

"See you in a couple of days for our first session Lakea", Dr. Roth said leaving the room.

Lakea laid there and drifted off into a dream of her future. A future where she was happy again and everything was okay. In this dream she had a family, a lot of kids, and a tall handsome husband with deep mysterious eyes. In this dream Lakea was happy and loved. She hoped that the dream would come true, but she knew that with her luck and how struggles loved to find her, she was sure that reaching happiness would not be easy.

However, she was willing to work to get it.

Once Lakea left the hospital, Ray-Ray fulfilled his promise and took her to her truck and house. Lakea was happy and amazed by the beautiful cream and brick house she now had. She was also happy to find that Jeremy had decorated the inside of the three- bedroom home just as he thought she would want it. Her living room was all black with framed pictures of Angela Davis, Foxy Brown, Billy Holiday, and Etta James covering the walls. There was nice black, leather furniture, a huge fish tank, and a fireplace. Her den was nice too and very cozy. A round, burgundy, sectional sofa sat in the middle of the floor, there was a 62" plasma TV on the wall in front of the couch, a fish tank that stretched all around the room, and a soft plush rug that covered the beautiful hardwood floor. Lakea couldn't help but cry as she walked past and touched the huge, wall-sized picture of her and Jeremy that hung over the couch.

"It's okay lil sis, the pain will get better." Ray-Ray said hugging his sister.

At that moment Lakea looked into her brother's eyes and for the first time, she saw the pain that he felt too. She hugged her brother tighter and told him that she loved him. They both hugged each other and cried as they thought about the loves they had lost.

Lakea and Ray-Ray continued to walk through the house looking at all that Jeremy had done. Upon further inspection of the house Lakea saw that Jeremy had even set up her bedroom, the nursery, and the guest room. She couldn't believe all of the thought, time, energy, and money Jeremy had put into the house making sure that she would be able to live well.

"I haven't been here but once lil sis. I didn't know about all of this." Ray-Ray said as they entered the nursery and stared at the mural Jeremy had painted on the walls and ceiling.

It was a beautiful jungle scene with colorful, exotic birds, giraffes, monkeys, and elephants. At the top of the wall was a beautiful sky with Lakea and Jeremy's faces faded into the background, and the ceiling was covered in stars. It was absolutely beautiful. Lakea started to weep again just looking at Jeremy's face and knowing that he had used his talent to leave something behind for his child.

"Come on lil sis." Ray-Ray said grabbing Lakea's arm and leading her out of the room as she grabbed a teddy bear out of the crib.

It was a cute and cuddly bear with bright red overalls on and for some reason the bear reminded Lakea of Jeremy. Lakea held the teddy bear tightly to her heart as she let her brother guide her to the master bedroom across the hall. That room was beautiful too. There was a king-sized bed with a pillow headboard and matching dresser with mirror and nightstand against the far wall. A rocker glider chair sat in the corner by the window, next to a bookshelf filled with books. A big screen TV was mounted to the wall across from the bed, and a large picture of Lakea and Jeremy on her 15th birthday hung over the bed. Lakea stared at the picture. They looked so innocent then, so full of love and hope. Tears began to stream down Lakea's face again.

"Lay down lil sis and rest, please. I'm going to go to the store and get you some groceries and anything else I think you may need. You just rest. I will stay with you as long as you need me too - but you know Mesha, Quan and Ray-Jay will be here later to keep you company." Ray-Ray said.

"Good. I need their love around me right now." Lakea said, sinking down under the soft, blue blanket on her bed and snuggling up with her teddy bear.

"I cannot wait to see my nephew Ray-Jay. By the way big bruh. Thank you!" Lakea said in a shaky voice.

"Know that I will always be here for you too - and I will always treat my nephew like he is my own." Lakea said staring up at her brother.

"Anytime lil sis. We all we got, remember?" Ray-Ray said kissing his sister on her forehead and leaving the room.

Lakea laid there looking around at everything when RayRay left, then she noticed a book on her bookshelf that stuck out more than the others. After getting up and retrieving the book, Lakea noticed that a letter was tucked inside. The outside of the envelope read, "To my love, know that I am always with you and that you mean the world to me."

Chapter 4

Suddenly Lakea felt weak and the room began to spin. She barely made it to the bed before her legs gave out and she fell back on to the bed. When Ray-Ray walked into her room a little while later he found her on the bed breathing hard and crying, still holding the letter.

"Lil sis, you have to pull yourself together." Ray-Ray said helping his sister to sit up. "You are going to make yourself sicker and that will affect the baby", Ray-Ray said.

Lakea knew that her brother was right, but she couldn't help but to be overcome with emotions every time she thought of Jeremy.

"What's that?" Ray-Ray asked, taking the letter out of Lakea's hand.

"It's a letter from Jeremy." Lakea said in a weak voice.

"You want me to open it?" Ray-Ray asked.

"No. I'm not ready to open it now." Lakea said as a tear fell from her eye and she took the letter back.

"Well don't open it until you are ready. But in the meantime sister, you have to pull yourself up. Remember what daddy always told us?" Ray-Ray said as he stood in front of his sister.

Lakea nodded her head yes and smiled slightly.

"Daddy always said being sad and self-pity gets you nowhere, so you have to be strong like Jeremy would have wanted you to be. Do you want the baby to be sick?" Ray-Ray asked Lakea as he pulled her up by her hands to her feet.

"No, of course not." Lakea said.

"Well, we're done with sadness then. You are about to get out of this house. We going to go baby shopping and have a good day. I can get you a Hover Round." Ray-Ray said, nudging his sister and encouraging her to smile.

She did and she felt a little better. Lakea knew that her brother was right. She had to snap back to reality and leave all the sadness behind her. She had to channel her anger again so that it could help her through this sadness, it always helped. Lakea tucked Jeremy's letter into the overalls of her teddy bear before she left the room, sucking up her sadness and stepping out on faith.

Over the next few days Lakea felt herself getting stronger and stronger. Her sadness was beginning to fade, and she was slowly returning to her old self. Her first individual therapy session with Dr. Roth went well. Lakea told her a little about her childhood, explaining how good life was when her daddy was still alive, how strong her mama was after his death, and how things changed for the worse when her mama met Jeff. Dr. Roth was very kind and understanding. She just listened to Lakea intently while writing on her pad. Then she would stop writing and look at Lakea with the most sympathetic eyes she had ever seen. Lakea could feel her compassion and understanding as she described the abuse she endured as a child, and how that abuse had manifested into destructive behaviors. That compassion and understanding Dr. Roth shared was exactly what Lakea needed at that time. She needed someone to listen and let her vent without judgment. Lakea's life up to that point had been so chaotic and violent, she needed the calmness that seeing Dr. Roth offered. Lakea hoped that somehow, she could gain some of those characteristics and begin to live a better, calmer, more normal life. She could finally be her true self.

When her hour session ended Lakea actually felt better because she knew that she was taking all of the necessary steps to move past the hurt and be complete. She was truly going to work hard to be a better person, so she thought. When she left the building, she decided to go spend some time with her favorite cousin Mesha at her friend Alana's house in the Shannon Falls Apartments in Frayser. She couldn't wait for her cousin to hear about the progress she was making. Lakea blasted Lauryn Hill's "Killing Me Softly" as she cruised down Frayser Blvd. Her mind was now all over the place. Her heart was still heavy from her loss, but her mind was torn between thoughts of hope and those of despair. She was so worried about what her future would be like. Lakea worried that she wouldn't be able to keep her house, feed her baby, or get pass all of her old demons. She worried that she and Felicia would never be as close as they should be. She also worried that she would always be that broken girl; that broken girl that her Jeff, her mama, and Klemmings had created.

By the time Lakea pulled up in front of Alana's building she had a new outlook on life. She was done being sad all of the time and she was done being the victim. Lakea decided she would suck all of the sad and hurt feelings she felt up and do what she had to do. No matter what she would keep a roof over her head and her baby and nephew would be taken care of. She knew that she had to be strong even if on the inside she was broken. When Lakea stepped out of the truck and the cool breeze blew up her dress she felt free. It was the beginning of August in Memphis, TN, so it was beyond hot, but the cool breeze coming off the Mississippi River that day made the heat tolerable. Lakea had on nothing under her blue and yellow sundress, as usual. She still loved to feel the breeze against her bare skin.

The pool in Alana's apartments was packed. Everyone wanted to be outside, but it was so hot that the pool was your only safe option. When Lakea stepped out of the car and walked on to the sidewalk she immediately heard her cousin Mesha's voice coming from the pool, so she made her way over there. Lakea was three and a half months pregnant at this point, her little stomach poked out through her dress, but she was still cute. As she approached the fence surrounding the pool Lakea saw her cousin and Alana standing with their backs to the fence ready to fight. Mesha was yelling and taunting three girls who were yelling back at her from the other side of a row of lawn chairs. About two dozen neighborhood boys and girls were running around the two groups of girls with their camera phones out.

"Whoop that bitch!" A boy with a camcorder yelled as he ran pass taping the altercation.

"Wasup with y'all pussy ass hoes?" Mesha yelled as she threw one of the patio chairs at the girls.

Lakea picked up her pace and burst through the fence going off. She had forgotten she was pregnant and that she was trying to change her life. All she knew was three girls were trying to hurt her cousin and she couldn't let that happen. Lakea was back to the old her in that instant.

"Maine, wasup cousin?!" Lakea yelled as she walked up to Mesha and Alana while wrapping her long key chain with the metal balls and spikes on it around her hand.

"These maggot ass hoes hot cause they niggas choosing. Fat hoodbooga bitches!" Mesha said as the girls yelled a slew of, "Bitches" and "Hoes", but did not advance pass the row of chairs.

"Maine, we ain't finna argue with you pussy ass hoes. Y'all bitches better swerve foe this shit get serious!" Lakea said, trying to diffuse the situation, in her own subtle way.

"Shut the fuck up bitch. We fight pregnant hoes too!" One of the three girls with a loudmouth yelled.

"These hoes obviously don't know me cousin." Lakea said turning from her cousin back to the girls.

Just then the big and tall girl of the group ran up and tried to punch Lakea in the face. However, the girl didn't count on Lakea still being fast and light on her feet despite her baby bump. Lakea quickly dodged the girl's punch and followed it with a right hook right to the girl's temple. The chain on Lakea's fist cut through the girl's flesh, splitting her face on impact. Blood squirted all over Lakea's face, hands, and arms. She looked like Carrie as she kneed the girl in the stomach while holding her by her hair and slamming her on the ground.

All mayhem broke loose at that point. Mesha beat one of the girls with a lawn chair as Alana drug the loudmouth girl by her hair and stomped her. After Lakea got the big girl on the ground she started to get on top of her so could pound her face in, only the girl started kicking wildly. The girl kicked Lakea so hard in her stomach that she went flying back into the fence. The impact of the blow made her whole-body shake. The sight of Lakea laying there pregnant and shaking caused the crowd to erupt. They pushed forward cursing, kicking, and stomping the girl who was balled up in the fetal position on the ground. Lakea was in so much pain all over, but all she could think of was her baby.

"My baby, what have I done?" Lakea yelled as two of Alana's male friends picked her up and carried her to her truck.

After seeing her cousin being carried away Mesha went crazy. She broke through the crowd and jumped on top of the girl delivering punch after punch to the girl's face and head. Soon blood was all over Mesha's face and hands as she continued to punch the girl with no mercy. Blood squirted out of the girl's nose and mouth and she moaned in pain. After a few more seconds and a couple more punches, Mesha ran to the truck screaming her cousin's name.

"Is she okay?" Mesha asked the two guys as they cradled Lakea's head through the door of the backseat.

One of the boys took of his icy white t-shirt and wiped the blood off Lakea's face and hands and then started to do the same to Mesha. Mesha stared at Lakea, laying in the back seat with blood splattered down her dress.

"Whose blood is that? Is she OK??" Mesha yelled frantically rushing towards the driver seat.

"She hurt but she okay." the boy who had taken his shirt off said as he and the other boy got out of the truck.

"You calm down. You want me to drive?" He asked Mesha after seeing how badly her hands were shaking.

"No!" Mesha said as she jumped into the driver's seat and sped out of the parking lot.

"You gone be okay." Mesha said to her cousin looking into the rear-view mirror.

"Please don't let me lose my baby!" Lakea cried.

"He all I got. Please, please, please", Lakea continued to cry and plead as Mesha sped down Thomas Street towards The Med.

Lakea prayed that her baby was alright. She couldn't believe that something so tragic was happening to her again, and so soon. Lakea cried hysterically in the back seat until she suddenly passed out from the stress halfway to the hospital.

"KEA!!" Mesha yelled as she glanced at her cousin through the rear-view mirror.

Mesha prayed that her cousin and the baby would be alright, but things didn't look good.

Chapter 5

Mesha got Lakea to the hospital in less than 8 minutes. She sped through every red light and cut downside streets, dodging terrible Memphis drivers and potholes. Mesha was really becoming a great driver in an emergency situation. She got her cousin to the hospital quickly and safely, although she was frantic on the inside.

As Mesha sat in the waiting room she couldn't help but feel sorry for her cousin. She had been through so much already, from doing three years in jail, watching her true love being murdered, being shot herself, and coming out of a coma to find out she was pregnant. Now she was in the hospital, possibly about to lose her baby. Not to mention all of the neglect, hurt, and abuse from her past. Mesha couldn't imagine going through all of the struggles her cousin had gone through. She couldn't imagine how her cousin had stayed so strong for so long.

Mesha sat there with her head down feeling guilty and praying that Lakea was alright. After about 45 more minutes a doctor came out and told Mesha that Lakea was doing fine and that she could go in the back to see her. When Mesha entered the room Lakea sat there in the bed, holding her stomach with tears in her eyes.

"Are you okay cousin?" Mesha asked sitting down next to her and grabbing her hand.

"Yes, we alright. They did an ultrasound, and the baby looks fine. Thank God." Lakea said holding her stomach and shaking her head.

"We think it's a boy. The doctor said that even though I put some unnecessary stress on the baby's heart today, he is doing fine - but I will have to be placed on a lot of physical limitations. He said I need to reduce my emotional stress too. That's going to be damn near impossible with all I'm dealing with." Lakea said looking out of the window as a little blue bird landed on the window seal and began staring inside.

Lakea stared back and she felt strength.

"I'm going to try though cousin." Lakea said turning back to her cousin as the little bird flew away.

"And I'm going to help you." Mesha said smiling at her cousin through her tears.

Mesha did help her cousin as she always had done. That evening she drove Lakea home, made them dinner, and then helped her into bed. They both lie there together after dinner and watched Love & Basketball until Lakea began to weep. That was her and Jeremy's favorite movie to watch together. Lakea held her teddy bear close to her and ran her fingers over Jeremy's letter.

"When are you going to open it?" Mesha asked.

"I don't know cuzzo, when I feel ready, I guess", Lakea said, closing her eyes and resting her head on her cousin's shoulder as she drifted off into a sweet dream about her one true love.

The next couple of days were good for Lakea. Mesha stayed with her the entire time, and Felicia, Quan, Ray-Ray, and Aunt Violet were there almost every day. Lakea was also spending a lot more time with her nephew Ray-Jay. He was stuck to her like glue wherever she went. Lakea loved the family time, but she only wished it could have happened under different circumstances.

Three days after Lakea's close call was her first group session with Dr. Roth and ten other grieving women. Lakea wasn't so sure about sitting in a circle with other sad bitches and having to tell her story, but she was willing to give it a try for her baby's sake. She arrived at Dr. Roth's office about 15 minutes late that afternoon, so all of the other ladies were already in their seats sharing by the time Lakea walked in. Dr. Roth was using one of the large offices on the second floor of her building on 100 N. Main for her group meetings. Lakea was used to going to her small cozy office on the third floor. This room was huge, bright, and white. There were 12 cushy chairs placed in a circle in the middle of the room. On the dry mark erase board in the front of the room the words: **Learn to Let Hurt Go and Love Yourself. There is Life After Death**! It was written in big bold letters. Lakea felt those words were just for her and she couldn't keep her eyes off of the board as she walked to her seat. She was so caught up in those words and what they meant she wasn't paying attention and bumped right into the lady next to her as she sat down.

"Sorry." Lakea said sitting down.

She still didn't look at the person, her attention was still on the dry mark erase board. When Lakea heard the lady say,

"No problem.", she knew that it was going to be a problem, she knew that voice. Lakea snapped her head around quickly to see the lady she had bumped into and it was no other than her worst enemy. The girl who had taken so much from her, Tia! Lakea instantly jumped to her feet as Tia did the same.

"Bitch!" Is the only word Tia got out of her mouth before Lakea wrapped her hands around her throat and they began to tussle.

All the women in the group screamed and jumped out of the way. Dr. Roth immediately sprang into action grabbing Lakea.

"You know what just happened with your baby!" Dr. Roth yelled as her and three other ladies pulled Tia and Lakea apart.

"Why do you all hate each other so much?" Dr. Roth asked as she held Lakea back.

"She's the one who caused all the tragedy in my life!" Lakea yelled with tears rolling down her cheeks.

"This is the girl I was telling you about, the one who tried to take Jeremy from me and got her brother to attack me, so Jeremy had to protect me. Then she sent him to kill me, and Jeremy protected me. Everything is all her fault!" Lakea yelled while lunging forward trying to hit Tia.

"It's my fault?" Tia yelled breaking away from the woman holding her and standing in front of Lakea.

"I'm not going to hit her, I see she pregnant." Tia said to the women who were grabbing her and then turned back to Lakea.

"I ruined YOUR life? Bitch, you stole my entire life. It's because of YOU I was kicked out of school after the fight and I didn't graduate. It's because of YOU my brother is gone. He was my everything and YOU took him away from me!" Tia said hitting herself in the chest as she talked with tears running down her face. "He was the only person besides my little sister who loved me!" Tia sobbed.

"My mama was on drugs. All I had was my brother, and after he died my life ended. My mama just got ghost, leaving me and my little sister alone so we had to go to the state. A year later my little sister was adopted, and I haven't seen her since. I don't even know if she is in Tennessee or if her name is the same. I haven't seen my mama in five years, I don't know if she is alive or dead. So, I ask you who ruined whose life?" Tia asked crying hysterically.

For the first time Lakea saw Tia as a real person and she realized that they had more in common than she had ever imagined.

"See, this is great progress." Dr. Roth said as both girls stood inches apart staring at each other with pain and hurt in their eyes.

"At least you both can see how you have hurt each other, and now maybe you all can begin to move past it. I don't expect you all to be best friends or anything like that, but you two do have to forgive one another so that those broken hearts can begin to heal." Dr. Roth said taking them both by the hand and returning them to their seats.

They both stared at each other for a minute after sitting down. Tears were on both of their cheeks.

'Maybe I can forgive her. I did forgive Felicia after all she did to me. Maybe our stories are the same.' Lakea thought to herself.

Lakea didn't know it then, but Tia's story was very similar to hers. She found that out over the next few weeks in therapy. Tia revealed her own demons to the group as everyone sat in with a familiar pain in their eyes. Tia told stories involving her being sold by her mother to dope boys since the age or six and being abuse by her mother. When her mother was high on crack, which was almost every day, she would become violent and beat Tia and her little sister. That's why her brother Red was her everything, he would protect them. One time she had even knocked Tia's two front teeth out with an iron because she said she talked back. Tia's life just like Lakea's had been no fairytale. They both quickly realized that after they had each heard the others story.

The next couple of weeks went by fast and the girls began to share more and more of their sorted pasts and found various similarities. The animosity that had grown between them over the years was slowly fading, and they were learning to put their differences aside. They both had already lost so much, they had to at least try to reach that level of peace and tranquility Dr. Roth said would come with forgiveness. So, one day towards the end of the group sessions when Lakea was eight and a half months pregnant Tia approached her as she wobbled into the room.

"Hey!" Tia said looking down. I just wanted to let you know that...I'm sorry." Tia said in tears.

"I'm sorry too." Lakea said as the tears welled up behind her eyes, and then she and Tia hugged.

Both broken girls were taking the steps necessary to be whole again. Lakea smiled. It felt good to let go of that part of her past and move forward. She knew that she and Tia wouldn't magically become best friends or no shit like that, but at least they didn't have to hate and blame each other anymore.

After that Lakea was excited to go to therapy. They were helping her so much. Her individual therapy was helping her to deal with all of her emotions related to the losing Jeremy, being pregnant, and learning how to heave a healthy relationship with her mama. Her group therapy was helping her to see that she was not alone and deal with the demons of her past. That therapy was helping Lakea to see that tragedy happened to everyone. Lakea wondered what her family therapy would reveal. She couldn't stop thinking about what her daddy had said to her about her mama having a secret. She wondered what the secret was and what it would do to her and her mother's already fragile relationship. She didn't have to wait long to find out though because her first family session with her mother was one week away, on the day she would turn 38 weeks.

Chapter 6

It was a cool February day - Valentine's Day to be exact - when Lakea pulled into the parking garage attached to Dr. Roth's office. She sighed to herself as she prepared to make her way to the elevator that would take her to the office on the third floor. The wind cut through her black pea coat, burgundy sweater dress, and black tights as she walked across the parking garage and to the elevator. Lakea tried to move fast to quickly get out of the cold, but the extra 50 pounds she was now carrying around made it difficult. Lakea munched on the huge stick of beef jerky she had in her hand as she entered Dr. Roth's office and greeted her mama in the waiting room. Lakea hadn't talked to her mama in the past three days, which was pretty unusual since everything had happened. She wondered was Felicia up to her old tricks. Had she found another kick-yo-ass-sit-on-yo-couch-and-live-off-you-beat-yo-ass-atrandom type of nigga to occupy her time again?

"Hey ma, where you been?" Lakea asked her mama, still eating her beef jerky while trying to make eye contact.

Felicia looked everywhere but at Lakea. Something was wrong, Lakea just couldn't figure out what it was.

"I haven't been feeling well baby. Something has been eating me up inside for a long time. I been trying to build up my courage to tell you that......" Felicia said looking at Lakea with tears in her eyes.

"Hello Ladies!" Dr. Roth interrupted as she walked out of her office.

"Are you ladies ready?" Dr. Roth asked smiling until she saw the looks on their faces.

Lakea looked confused, while Felicia looked as if her whole world was crumbling.

"Is everything okay? Are you ladies ready for today?" Dr. Roth asked as she held the door to her office open and encouraged the women to enter.

"I'm about ready as I will ever be." Felicia said walking into the office. Then suddenly she stopped and turned to Lakea who was entering the room behind her. "I just hope, no… I pray that everything is still ok with us after I tell you what I have to say." Felicia said, and then she turned and took her seat.

Lakea followed dazed. She didn't know what to expect and she couldn't stop the aching feeling she had in her heart. Dr. Roth sighed softly then entered the room closing the door behind her. Lakea couldn't take her eyes off of Felicia as she took her seat. She wondered what the secret was that her mother was hurting so much over. They had already suffered through so much; she wondered what could be this bad and how the information might affect her.

"Ladies… so who would like to begin?" Dr. Roth asked sitting down and clasping her hands on her hands together on her desk.

"I will begin." Felicia said turning in her chair to face Lakea.

"Baby I know that there is no excuse for some of the things that I have done and allowed to be done in your life, but I want you to know that I am deeply sorry for it all. If I could turn back the hands of time I would, because I love you and your brothers with all of my heart", Felicia said.

Lakea looked intensely at her mama as she spoke, lingering on her every word. She couldn't imagine what her mother was about to say, but she had the feeling that the words Felicia were about to speak would change a lot. She had the feeling that what her mama would tell her would change who she was.

"To fully understand why I have been so selfish and to understand why back then I didn't know how to love anyone, I will have to tell you everything, from the beginning!" Felicia said with tears in her eyes.

"I was once a very special girl, the sparkle in my daddy's life. Being the youngest of three boys and three girls, I was daddy's little princess. I could do no wrong. Well..." Felicia said with a faraway look in her eyes as she turned her head and stared out of the window. "Daddy died when I was 11 and I became the outcast, the black sheep. Mama was never around. She was always at work, so we raised each other. My sisters were mean, and my brothers were just concerned with themselves. Nothing I did or said mattered. During that time in my life, I was always lonely and so trusting, which led to me being molested by my best friend's father from the age of 11 to 14. I never told anyone, because it wouldn't matter if I did." Felicia said as her voice cracked, and tears welled up in her eyes.

"When I was 16, I finally moved out on my own and soon I met Marvin and we had Rasheed." Felicia continued.

By this time, the tears were falling from Lakea's eyes. She could feel her mama's pain and this unspoken connection that some rape victims share. Lakea knew that her mama knew how it felt to be hurt so bad you don't want to go on, which is why she found it ridiculous that her mama did nothing to stop it from happening to her. Just as Lakea was about to ask her mama that question she answered it.

"I was weak baby. That's why I didn't stop it. I didn't want to believe that it was happening. I was so caught up in my own pain that I was oblivious to yours." Felicia said turning back facing Lakea and pulling her chair closer to her as she grabbed her hand. "Baby I couldn't love or make good decisions back then when you needed me most, just like I couldn't when I was with Marvin."

Lakea sat there stunned. She couldn't figure out why her mama kept referring to her daddy as Marvin and what she meant when she said she couldn't make good decisions then. Back then she was perfect in Lakea's eyes, so she knew this secret was deep. She braced herself in her seat swallowing down the beef jerky that was creeping back up her throat. Lakea didn't have to wonder what her mother's secret was long because the next words Felicia spoke shattered all she ever knew.

"Well baby, all of the events of my childhood led me to drugs. For the first two years of Ray-Ray's life baby, I was addicted to cocaine." Felicia said with shameful eyes.

Lakea couldn't believe it. Her mother was so perfect and loving back then. Lakea didn't want to taint that perfect family picture she had in her head. That was the hope she held for the future. Lakea shook her head no as the tears continued to run down her face.

"It's true baby. I was good at hiding it from your daddy and everyone else until one day when Ray-Ray was about to turn 1 someone found out. He threatened to tell Marvin. I knew that news would devastate him and end everything we had so when he offered a solution, I agree without thinking. He wanted me to be his personal side piece and in return he would keep my secret and supply me with the drugs." Felicia said through her tears.

Lakea sobbed loudly. She never imagined her mama was addicted to a drug like cocaine, and when her daddy was still alive at that.

Felicia went on. "So, I began sleeping with him behind your da... Marvin's back whenever he asked...until the unthinkable happened." Felicia said standing.

"Ma, why do you keep calling my daddy Marvin - and what happened?" Lakea asked crying.

Her heart was beating so fast she thought it would jump out of her chest.

"I became pregnant with his baby, not my husband's. Marvin found out shortly after the baby was born, but he didn't care. We remained together and had another child." Felicia said, finally looking Lakea in the eyes.

"What?" Lakea and Dr. Roth both asked with a confused look on their faces.

Lakea couldn't believe her ears. Where was the baby her mother had by another man?

"Lady bug, that baby I had by another man was you! Baby, Marvin wasn't your daddy." Felicia cried.

Those words made Lakea's heart drop. She immediately felt as if she would be sick, and the room began to spin. Her body began to tremble, and her face was covered in sweat.

"Who is my daddy mama?" Lakea asked, crying hysterically as Dr. Roth came around the desk to hug her.

"I think that may be enough for today Felicia." Dr. Roth said sternly as Lakea continued to cry and tremble.

"No, Dr. Roth. I have to tell her this. Jacob baby, Jacob is your daddy." Felicia yelled.

Suddenly, everything went black again. Those were the last words that Lakea heard before she fainted.

"Jacob is your DADDY!"

Chapter 7

When Lakea woke up at The Med Labor and Delivery Felicia was right there by her side. The words, "Jacob is your father.", still rang in her ears as tears fell from her eyes. Lakea delivered a 9 lb. 2 oz. healthy, baby boy. He was so handsome and so big.

"He is going to be a heart-breaker", Felicia said holding her second grandson Jeremy Jaquan Mitchell, Jr.

Jeremy had left paperwork ensuring his son would have his name. It seems he had covered all of the bases. That made Lakea happy knowing that he cared so much for his baby without even knowing him. Felicia handed Lakea J-J and she fell in love at first sight. He was so chubby and so happy already. He had gray eyes just like Jeremy, except they were almond shaped just like hers. His complexion was golden brown, and he had a head full of thick curly hair and long, thick eyelashes. He was the perfect combination of Lakea and Jeremy. He was everything beautiful, pure, and innocent about them. Lakea felt nothing but love as she held her baby. All of the anger and hurt she carried around with her disappeared in that moment and she felt nothing but unconditional love and hope.

As Lakea stroked his hair, J-J looked directly up into her eyes and she felt a love and connection she never dreamed possible.

"Mommy loves you more than anything baby. My J-J!" Lakea said as she kissed her son's forehead and held him tight while glancing at her mama.

"I'm sorry baby", Felicia began, but Lakea cut her off.

"It is what it is mama. Marvin was the only daddy I ever knew and that is that. A lot of things have happened in my life - some good, most bad - but I'm still here. And I'm still here for a purpose. I just found that purpose." Lakea said looking down at her son.

"I'm going to the best mama that I can be to my son. The mama you never were to me - and in order for me to do that I have to let everything go. So, mama I love you, and I forgive you. Okay?" Lakea said looking back up at her mother.

Felicia stood there crying as Lakea wiped the tears from her eyes.

"I forgive you mama, so let's just move forward. Can we do that?" Lakea asked.

Felicia shook her head yes as she kissed her daughter's hand, and they did just that. They moved forward to a brighter day.

Things were good for them all for about a year after that. Lakea got a customer service job at a local cable company, which helped her to keep her house and car. Felicia got herself together too and moved close to Lakea to help with J-J and Ray-Jay. Ray-Ray moved in with Lakea after he met a girl named Jessica soon after J-J was born. Jessica was now nine months pregnant with Ray-Ray's second son,

Rahiem. Lakea had a house full with herself, her son, her nephew Ray-Jay, her brother RayRay, and his pregnant girlfriend. It was like the damn Brady Bunch. Quan had just finished high school at the top of his class and was preparing to go to college at Morehouse in the fall.

Everything was going well for everyone until Jessica had a heart attack while giving birth to Rahiem. Ray-Ray was devastated. He totally checked out of life even though he had two sons to take care of. That left everything on Lakea. Jessica had been from Texas with no living family since her parents died in a car accident when she was 13, so Lakea was now Rahiem's provider too. Lakea had to be mama and daddy for her son and both of her nephews all while fighting her demons.

After Jessica's funeral Ray-Ray totally disappeared, lost in his grief. He quit his job at UPS and people from the hood told Lakea that they saw him walking the streets drunk and high. Lakea searched for him for days and couldn't find him. She hoped he would come back and help her because she was under so much pressure and things were not getting better. No matter how much overtime she put in at the cable company, she never seemed to make enough to cover all of her expenses. Felicia helped out when she could but that wasn't much.

"Call Jacob." Felicia told Lakea one day when she called her mama asking for gas money.

"He owes you so many years of child support; I know for sure he will help you." Felicia said.

"Hell no. I don't need it that bad." Lakea said sucking her teeth.

Although she had forgiven her mama, she wasn't sure she wanted to forgive Jacob just yet; her favorite uncle. The one who betrayed her daddy and lied to her all of her life. No, she wasn't ready to ask him for anything yet.

"I'll get it." Lakea said before hanging up with her mama.

Lakea did get the money after going to the blood bank and making a donation for $35. She felt so low and worthless sitting in the blood bank with all of the bums and junkies in there donating to get a fix. However, she had to do what she had to do. It was Friday, pay day - and she had to have enough gas to get to work and to Walmart after work to cash her check, so she sucked it up and did it.

At work Lakea was hit with another sack of bullshit when her check was $150 short. She forgot she was late three times in the last week and had to leave early twice when her sitter fell through. Now she was going to pay for it by receiving a little as check that wouldn't cover her rent, which was due the following Monday. Not to mention she needed food and had to pay the kids day care bill the next Friday. Everything seemed to be crashing down on her at one time.

Lakea sat there at her desk in a daze, worried about what she would do. Just then her cell phone went off. It was a text from her cousin Mesha.

What are you doing junt? Mama want to watch the boys tonight and I want you to come party with me. Sooooo HOE, come over here when you leave that lame ass job.

Lakea smiled to herself while reading her cousin's text. It had been a while since she had kicked it with her cousin Mesha. Hell, it had been a while since she had done anything except work and take care of the boys. Lakea wanted to get out. She needed to get out because she could feel herself falling back into depression. She was thinking more and more about Jeremy as she sat at home alone each night, worrying about bills and how she would care for the boys.

I'm down BITCH! Lakea texted back to Mesha, followed by another text. **I'm fucked up. I need some money asap.**

Mesha texted back in seconds.

I got you; I got just the hustle you need.

Lakea smiled and actually felt a little better. She knew that whatever her cousin was on involved tricking, stripping, or robbing a nigga, but she didn't care at that point. She knew she would get the money she needed and that's all that mattered. She was trying to survive.

The rest of Lakea's workday breezed by with ease. When it was time to clock out at 6:30 p.m., Lakea was actually skipping out of the building. She was ready to enjoy her night worry-free for a change. She rushed to Walmart and cashed her check then sped to pick up the boys. When she pulled up at Hands on Learning Enrichment Center bumping India Arie's, "The Truth" she felt a sense of peace from the chaos of her life. That song always made her think of her good times with Jeremy and how much love she had for him. Lakea was still singing the lyrics to the song when she walked through the door. Ray-Jay met her at the door squealing. "Here go my Te-Te, I miss my Te-Te!"

Lakea swept him up off his feet and covered his face in kisses like his daddy always did her. J-J wobbled up behind Ray-Jay yelling, "Ma." with a huge smile on his face. Lakea swooped him up in her other arm and covered his face in kisses too as he giggled. She stared into his chocolate face for a second, lost in his beautiful eyes. She loved her son so much and she loved looking at his handsome face. He was the mirror image of his father, just smaller.

After putting the boys down Lakea gathered their things, got baby Rahiem, and prepared to leave the day care. She was trying to avoid Kizzy, the day care director because she knew she owed her money. Just as she made it out of the door to the boy's classroom Kizzy popped out of the room next door and stopped her.

"Damn!" Lakea said under her breath as Kizzy stood there with her hands on her hips and a sour look on her face.

"Uh huh, I caught your ass didn't I. Now look Lakea I know things are rough for single parents, hell I'm one too, and I know that you have your brother's kids too - but I'm running a business honey, so I'm gone need my money by Friday in full No Exceptions!" Kizzy said trying to look caring but stern.

Lakea sighed deeply and shook her head.

'Here go the bullshit again.' Lakea thought to herself.

She knew that she owed the girl for three weeks, but damn she was hounding her forgetting all the free hairstyles she had gotten in the past.

"I know Kizzy, but I promise I got you. I may have it sooner than next Friday." Lakea said holding Rahiem in one arm and J-J in the other as Ray-Jay followed them out of the door.

"Why don't you get on welfare and then you can get free childcare?" Kizzy asked as she followed Lakea out to the car and helped her get the boys into their seats and buckled up.

Lakea sucked her teeth loudly and rolled her eyes at Kizzy. She was grateful for her advice, but now she was losing her mind. Over the past few months Lakea had grew close to Kizzy and they had become good friends, so she was always ready to tell Lakea what to do in any situation. They shared a common deep secret, a familiar sadness, a similar pain, which is why Lakea valued Kizzy's advice. Kizzy too had lived through a tragedy and turned it into a positive situation for her and her children. Kizzy's boyfriend had been killed in front of her too. A rival gang found him at his aunt's house in Frayser with Kizzy and the kids. They kicked the door in and blew his face off in front of them all. So Lakea knew that Kizzy understood her pain and her struggle very well. Lakea did trust her advice though on most things, just not this. She didn't want to depend on the state for anything. She wanted to make it on her own.

"No, I can't do that honey. I don't do no damn welfare. I'm just not that chick, but believe me you will have your money." Lakea said getting into the driver's seat and starting her truck.

"I'mma holla at you later. The boys won't be here tomorrow though cause I ain't working this weekend and my auntie keeping them. I'm going have me some fun!" Lakea said popping her lips and snapping her fingers after turning back on her India Arie CD.

"Alright now junt, be safe!" Kizzy yelled over the music as Lakea honked her horn and pulled off.

Chapter 8

The entire ride to her auntie's house, Lakea kept contemplating what should she do. Something was telling her to go home, not to start this pattern again, but she wasn't listening. She needed the money. As Lakea parked in her aunt Violet's driveway, she was overcome with sadness as the lyrics to India Arie's. "Good Man" blasted through her speakers.

"If the sun comes out and I'm not home be strong. If I'm not beside you do your best to carry on. Tell the kids about me when they're old enough to understand. Tell them that their daddy was a Good Man!" India Arie sung as tears ran down Lakea's face while she sat in her aunt's driveway and sobbed.

Just then Ray-Jay unbuckled himself and J-J, then he climbed into the front seat.

"Don't cry Te-Te." Ray Jay said using his little fingers to wipe away her tears as she kissed him on the head.

She then grabbed J-J as he climbed over the seat and hugged him tight while kissing his curly hair.

"I love you both." Lakea whispered to the boys who were both staring up at her with wide, teary eyes.

"I love you - and so do y'all daddies", Lakea wept.

The tears came harder and faster then. Lakea sat there and sobbed, holding her son until all of a sudden Mesha beat on the window.

"What's wrong June?" Mesha said snatching the car door open.

When she saw Lakea's tears and heard the song she was playing, which was now on repeat, she knew that everything was beginning to be too much for her cousin. Mesha grabbed Lakea around the neck and hugged her tight. She loved her big cousin so much. She was her inspiration of strength even though she had been through so much. However, Mesha was tired of her cousin being sad all the time. She wanted her to smile, have fun, and be free. After a few minutes of hugging and consoling her cousin Mesha abruptly stopped and stood up.

"Okay enough of this mushy, sadness shit! Come on! Cut this shit off first." Mesha said, turning of the engine so that the song would stop. "You have to stop listening to that song, you know it always makes you feel so depressed. Now, let's go get ready for tonight." Mesha said grabbing J-J out of Lakea's arms and opening the back seat door to get Rahiem out.

"You about to have some fun tonight and make some money, then Monday we gone really kill em. You gone be super bank and then you will be kissing my ass for hooking this up!" Mesha said rolling her eyes at Lakea.

"Ha, bitch you got some nerves. But what am I gone be kissing yo ass for? What are we doing?" Lakea asked wiping the tears from her eyes, grabbing Ray-Jay and her purse as she got out of the truck.

"You gone see skank. Just bring ya ass and get ready. You know me, so you know we fina be straight." Mesha said going into the house with Lakea following her inside.

Once inside the girls bathed and fed the boys then put them in the play area in the living room where Quan, MJ, Anterrius, and Anthony were playing the Xbox.

"Hey lil bruh." Mesha said, mushing Quan as she sat next to him on the couch.

"When do you have to leave for college Mr. Professional?" Lakea asked jokingly.

"I got one month, two weeks, and 3 days!" Quan said laughing.

"Damn fool, you sound like you getting out of jail." Anthony said laughing.

"Shiddd, Memphis is jail - or more like hell. And a muthafucka struggle e'rday trying to stay out that fire." MJ said as everyone laughed and agreed.

"Well, we having you a party before you leave." Lakea said, getting up and leaving the room.

When Lakea made it into Mesha's room she had already taken her shower and was sitting at her mirror doing her hair and makeup in a silk robe.

"Hooch, you better hurry up. I got some clothes for you. Just go take your shower and hurry the fuck up!" Mesha yelled waving her curl wand in the air.

"Can you tell me where we are going first so that I can mentally prepare?" Lakea asked as she gathered Mesha's robe and slippers to go take her shower.

"Okay, I guess I can go ahead and tell you. Monday, we gone do boxing at Purple Passion, but TONIGHT, we going to Satin and Sapphire to dance. Its amateur night, but I know for a fact that the Pilot Gang niggas and that Peer Pressure nigga gone be in the building, so you know they gone make it rain all night long." Mehsa said snapping her fingers and grinding her hips in her seat.

Lakea tried her best to smile, but her apprehension was on her face. Mesha could see it too as she stared at Lakea through the mirror as she brushed her long auburn hair.

"Bitch don't be scared, just be seductive and do this a lot." Mesha said swinging her long her from side-to-side while dipping down low and twerking her as cheeks up and down.

"You know how to do this; do like you did when we were in the room and you straight. Hell, you already fine and thick, so there's nothing to worry about. Okay?" Mesha asked.

"Okay. We gotta do what we gotta do right?" Lakea said faking a smile at her cousin and leaving the room.

As the hot water from the shower began to relax Lakea it also sent her back to a not so happy memory. Suddenly she was back locked up, behind the walls of Wolverine and Klemmings and his crew was having their way with her. She could still feel the sting of his riding whip on her back and hear the sound it made when it cut through the air. That was the same sound that had awakened her many nights, and now she would use that sound, that hate, that pain as her driving force to get her through her hard times. Lakea knew anger always pushed her and made her go harder so when she felt her anger start to rise at the memory of Wolverine and Klemmings she welcomed it. She remembered everything; all of the beatings she had to endure, being left naked and cold for days, being abused and humiliated by Klemmings and his crew as they forced her to have sex with them all in any way they wanted. She remembered it all.

By the time Lakea stepped out of the shower she was close to her old self again, well at least her anger and determination to manipulate and use as many men as she could had returned. She had been so wrapped up in her grief and pain from losing Jeremy; it had dulled that anger and pain of a broken little girl. However, now that anger was back, and she was ready to let it use her in any way it chose. As she wiped the steam off the mirror, Lakea took a good look at herself. She still saw a broken girl staring back at her through the mirror. However, the only difference was that now she didn't want to be broken. She knew she wanted to be whole again, and she knew that her future did not include dancing. She just had to figure how to pick up the pieces and mend her broken spirit.

Once Lakea and Mesha got dressed, Lakea looked in the mirror and felt more confident, ready to do what she had to. Mesha had straightened her long, thick black hair so that it was silky, and she did the prettiest, most seductive makeup on her with fake lashes and all. Lakea stared at herself in the mirror on Mesha's dresser and she couldn't believe what she saw. She looked just like one of those video girls. She had on a black corset top, black G-strings with black booty shorts on top, a black lace hi- low skirt, and her black, eight-inch red bottoms with the spikes. She was flawless in every way.

"Damn bitch you bad." Mesha said walking back into the room to get her purse.

"Bitch you ain't too shabby your damn self.", Lakea said looking at Mesha up and down.

She was flawless too in her black cat suit with diamond accents and diamond studded red bottom heels.

"We finna break these tricks." Mesha said looking in the mirror too as she put on more lip gloss and practiced puckering her lips. "Let's go pick up Nika and go get this money, you know she always down. Candius lame ass ain't going; you know she got a man now. She boo'd up!" Mesha said in a ghetto voice while rolling her neck.

"Must be nice", Lakea said as they left the room.

She wished that she could be boo'd up with Jeremy at that very minute and not have to go to the club and take her clothes off just to make rent. However, that wasn't her reality this was, so she had to try to make the best of it.

Lakea could feel the butterflies in her stomach rise up to her throat as they drove down Brooks Road, getting closer to Satin & Sapphire. Kush smoke filled the air as Lakea took a big hit of the blunt she had just lit. She hadn't smoked in a while, but she was trying to numb those guilty feelings that lingered, so she hit the blunt again extra hard. She knew that she had to detach herself from herself to pull off what she was about to do. The Kush and jug of lime Peer Pressure she was consuming was certainly doing the trick as she felt her feelings slowly fading. By the time they pulled into the club's parking lot, which was packed, Lakea felt warm, tingly, and very relaxed.

"Okay, I know y'all know how to do this." Mesha said looking at Lakea and Nika after parking and turning off the car.

"Hell yea bitch, I'm straight. I been striping in New Orleans the past month. I got this." Nika said as she puffed her Newport.

"Well, that's wasup bitch, we bout to bank. Lakea you ready?" Mesha asked looking at Lakea who now had a faraway look in her eyes.

"Ready as I'll ever be!" Lakea said turning to face her cousin and continuing.

"Bitch let's get this money. Fuck some feelings. I'm back on my break a trick shit. I got bills to pay." Lakea said, taking one last deep hit of the Kush trying to numb that bad feeling that still lingered within her.

"Now that's the shit I like. Let's go ladies!" Mesha said as they all got out of the car and made their way through the parking lot to the club.

The moon shone brightly as the girls walked to the side entrance of the club. Dudes were standing around staring at them looking like walking bags of money.

"Aye bitch, how much to fuck?" One of the guys standing by the front door yelled as the girls passed them.

"If you have to ask you probably can't afford it." Lakea said flipping her hair in his face like Mesha had told her to.

"Shidd, you can't put a price on perfection baby - and it don't get no better than this." Lakea said running her hands all over herself and she continued to go off on the dude. "So why don't you go get your lil baby bank up, then come holla at me!" Lakea said rolling her eyes.

All of the guys standing around erupted in a tirade of "Oohhh's" and checks. Even the dude's friends laughed, and that did not make him happy. Lakea could see it in his face.

"Damn, that's the boss bitch shit I'm talking about." Mesha said grabbing Lakea by one arm and Nika by the other, pulling them to the side door away from the dudes.

"I'mma do just that bitch, and you gone give me that pussy when I do...whether you want to or not!" The dude yelled staring at Lakea intently as he and his friends entered the club.

As the girls were standing at the door waiting on security to let them in Lakea looked up at the sky and all of the beautiful stars. She couldn't believe how beautiful the sky was, yet how ugly her life had become. She couldn't understand how her life always went from one extreme to the next, and she couldn't understand how she had gotten to where she now was, but she knew one thing. She would do whatever it took to ensure her son and nephews had what they needed, and if that meant stripping, so be it. Hell, she had already been through worse by no desire of her own. How bad could it be? If she only knew....

Chapter 9

When the side door to the club opened, Lakea swallowed that lump in her throat and went back into gangsta mode. She was the old Lakea again and it was time to break a trick, no time for feelings - and she planned on getting all that she could.

The inside of the club was smokey and dark as the girls entered. "Whistle While You Twerk", by the Ying Yang Twins blast through the club's huge speakers making Lakea cringe it was so loud. Strobe lights flashed different colors and guys were everywhere, in every seat yelling, smoking weed, and drinking. Girls walked around damn near naked and some of them were giving lap dances at tables. A tall, dark skinned, 400-lb man with a mean expression on his face met them at the door and ushered them to an office in the back of the club. Inside the office the girls sat down on one side of the huge oak desk and waited on the man to sit down.

"Okay, Mesha knows me, but y'all don't." the man said looking at Lakea and Nika as he sat down. "I'm Gator, and I am the manager of this club. Now I want y'all to know that I don't play no games. I expect you to work hard, and I will protect you. All y'all gotta do is do yo job, break these tricks and that's it!" Gator said in a serious tone.

"Now since y'all just wanna work from time-to-time Ima need a $65 pay out from each of you, either now or at the end of the night. Other than that, that it's just like every other strip club; $20 and up for table dances, $65 and up for a VIP, $20 of which comes to me. You gotta tip the DJ and security at the end of the night too. There is no fucking in the club, and no leaving the club with niggas to fuck or do parties. Y'all understand that?" Gator asked sitting behind the desk puffing his Cuban cigar with the same mean, expression on his face.

"Yeah." All of the girls said in unison as Lakea pulled $200 out of her bra while looking at Mesha.

"Take money to make money, right?" She said handing Gator two $100 bills.

He stared lustfully into her face then down to her neck and her titties, drinking her in with his eyes.

"You a beautiful lil bitch, I swear", he said handing her the $5 change.

"You gone make all the damn money and make all the hoes mad in the process. Shit, all y'all is wit y'all fine asses,"

Lakea smirked. "Well, we ain't worried about these hoes, just these tricks and they money. Right?" Lakea asked looking back at Mesha and Nika.

"Damn right!" They both yelled then laughed.

"That's what I'm talking about, true money makers. That's what I need in this muthafucka. Gone get that money then." Gator said standing. "Oh, here go a roll for all y'all. This will put ya right in the mood, forreal." Gator said as he handed each girl a little blue pill and a Smirnoff Ice from his mini fridge.

Lakea stared at the pill in her hand. She was kind of sacred because she had never taken ecstasy before, but she also had never stripped in a club before, so she figured it was a first time for everything. What better time than now. Besides, she did have to be someone else for the moment and that pill would definitely help her to morph into Kandi again. Each of the girls looked at each other as they stood in the doorway of the office.

"What you lookin at me for, I pop X all the time!" Mesha said scrunching her nose up at Lakea as she stared at her with disbelief on her face.

Lakea didn't know her cousin had done X before. Mesha shrugged and popped her pill in her mouth.

"Hell, I have done it before too. It ain't shit." Nika said as she swallowed her pill down.

"Fuck it!" Lakea said as she swallowed her pill down and they all entered the dressing room.

Lakea was totally surprised when she entered the dressing room with Mesha and Nika. It was nothing like she had imagined, there was no glitz or glamor. The left wall was filled with ugly off-gray lockers, the same colors as the walls, and most of them had broken doors with words written all over them. The floor was dirty and littered with empty condom wrappers, cigarette butts, baby wipes, and cigar tobacco. On the other wall was four large dirty mirrors hung above a long counter. There was a huge empty space where one of the mirrors was missing and girls had taped all kinds of pictures in that spot. Girls of all shapes and shades sat at the counter doing their hair, make-up, drugs, drinking, or simply talking shit. In the back there were three dirty bathroom stalls and a small, filthy shower in the corner. There was also a table and several chairs setup in the back, which a lady named Cutie, the house mama, had set up like a store. She had food, liquor, dance clothes, cigarettes, condoms, baby wipes, and any other thing a dancer might need including make-up application.

Mesha knew several girls in the club from doing parties the past couple of years, so many of them spoke as the girls took a seat at the counter on the far end of the dressing room. The girls began to touch up their makeup and hair as Lakea stared at each girl who passed in the mirror. She didn't trust females, at all. Besides, it was so noisy in the dressing room she had to watch everything. All of the girls that were still in the dressing room were high and loud. An older stripper everyone called Red, stood in the middle of the floor with a gallon jug of Vodka, butt naked telling stories and peeling other girls in between swigs of her alcohol.

"And look at these pretty bitches that just walked in!" Red yelled. "Y'all some siddity Beverly Hills 90210 bitches ain't it? Where you hoe from Harbor Town?" She asked laughing and wasting some of her liquor on the floor.

Some of the other girls laughed too and waved Red off.

"Aw that pretty, prissy bitch at the end look scared. That bitch ain't gone last." Red said pointing at Lakea while laughing.

Lakea scooted back in her chair. The old her was back and she was ready to fuck that drunk bitch up. Mesha knew what was about to happen so she grabbed her cousin's chair and pulled her back up to the counter, while whispering in her ear.

"Maine fuck that drunk, old bitch. Let that hoe talk while we run circles around her old antique ass." Mesha said.

Lakea laughed out loud because Mesha had caught her off guard with that comment, but it did put her back in a good mood.

"Fuck bitches, get money." Lakea said as she rolled her eyes at Red and turned back to the mirror to fix her makeup.

Just then a tall, dark skinned girl with blonde hair approached them. "Hey." the girl said touching Lakea on the shoulder.

"Wassup?" Lakea asked standing and taking a defensive posture.

She wasn't about to play with nobody in that damn club. She already had a familiar feeling of hostility like she felt when she got to Wolverine. It was too many females, so she knew trouble was lurking and she was ready. It was like her mama always told her. "Stay ready to keep from having to get ready." Mesha and Nika were ready too because they stood up as soon as Lakea did. They were her real ride or die's, always ready for whatever.

"Damnnn, it ain't like that y'all." the girl said laughing.

"That prissy bitch gone sprinkle fairy dust all over your ass Fantasy", Red said as her and the other girls continued laughing.

"I just wanted to see did I know you. Ain't yo name Lakea and didn't you go to Fairley?" The girl asked and Lakea began to relax, leaning on the counter.

Mesha and Nika sat back down and continued getting ready.

"You can never be too sure." Lakea said laughing. "But yeah, I went there,"

Lakea stared at the girl and suddenly her face became familiar. It was her friend from middle school, Makina. The girls hugged and laughed. They talked for a few minutes before Makina was called to the stage.

"Well, I will catch you later." Makina said as she began to leave the dressing room.

"Y'all hoes better be cool, cause this hoe jacking and Red you know you can't fight. Hell, that's Jeremy girl. Y'all know wassup." Makina said rolling her eyes at Red who quickly followed her out of the dressing room.

The sound of Jeremy's name made Lakea shudder, and she almost lost her nerve. She didn't want to think about him at that moment. She just wanted to do what she had to. The girls finished getting ready then Mesha stood up and told them it was time to hit the floor.

"You want to go by yourself or tag-along with me?" Mesha asked Lakea, standing in the door.

Lakea didn't want to stop her hustle so she told her and Nika to go and that she would figure it out on her own.

"Make that money junt!" Mesha said leaving out of the door with Nika close behind her.

Lakea stood there in front of the mirror admiring herself. She still couldn't believe how good she looked and now she had certain laid-back swag from the X that made her think she looked extra sexy. She did look exotic and seductive as she had taken off the high low skirt and just left on her booty short, corset, and heels.

"Bitch you bad as hell." Lakea heard from behind her as a tall, super thick red-bone girl sat down next to her.

She was really pretty with big brown eyes and full lips. Her ass and titties were HUGE too, which made Lakea fully understand how she was referred to as the top money maker in the club.

"I can tell you nervous, but you gone be straight. I'm Benzi by the way." the girl said.

"Wasup." Lakea said back.

"You got a stage name yet lil mama - cause you definitely gone need to hit that stage. That's where all the real money at." Benzi said.

Lakea thought for a second, might as well use the name I used before.

"Kandi!" Lakea said sitting on the counter and looking at Benzi.

"Okay that's a good name. Is this your first time?" Benzi asked as she lit her Kush blunt.

Lakea gave Benzi a quick rundown of her stripping resume as they puffed and passed the blunt back and forth. Lakea didn't know why, but she instantly trusted Benzi and knew that her expertise could help her through the night.

"I got you sexy ass lil girl. We gone go on stage together and you can stay with me until you feel comfortable." Benzi said getting up and walking to the door.

"You coming?" She said as she turned and looked at Lakea still standing staring in the mirror.

"Yea ma'am, leggo!" Lakea said as she followed Benzi out of the dressing room and into the lion's den.

The two of them dominated the room very quickly taking several girls' table dances and getting at least a $20 tip from each table, dance or not. By the time it was their turn to go on stage both Lakea and Benzi had made over $400, and they hadn't even done any VIP's, just dances; some for as much as $80. Mesha and Nika met Lakea in the dressing room as she was changing out of her booty shorts back into her skirt over her G-string so that she could easily get out of her clothes on stage.

"Bitch, it's too much money out there." Mesha said throwing her money bag on the counter, which had bills spilling out.

They each had made well over $1200 after doing table dances, VIP's, and going on stage once. They were naturals; however, Lakea was still a little more reserved and apprehensive.

"You gone be okay cuzzo, you can't fuck up. Hell, all the niggas tipping you already. I saw that Peer Pressure nigga give you a $100 tip for nothing." Mesha said flipping her hair at Lakea.

Lakea looked in the mirror at herself now on her fourth blunt, second drink, and second X pill. She wasn't afraid of dancing, hell they had done that as girls and got money - and besides her second pill had just kicked in so she was feeling beyond sexy. No, what she was afraid of was deeper than that. She was afraid that she was beginning to like this lifestyle and she didn't want to. She was afraid she would get hooked on the fast money and abundance of drugs and lose herself at that damn club.

"June you okay?" Mesha asked her, rolling a blunt.

"I'm straight cuzzo", Lakea said taking a sip out of her cup of Hennessy.

She was trying to calm the butterflies. Just then Benzi walked through the door.

"That bitch ain't scared of the stage, her ass scared she was made for this shit. I can see it in your eyes." Benzi said standing next to Lakea in the mirror and wiping her pussy with a baby wipe. "Hoe, that fear is normal. Most good bitches go through this they first time, but it's some nasty hoes that don't care."

"Meeee!" Red yelled as she pulled herself up on her locker laughing and wobbled out of the dressing room.

Benzi shook her head while smiling and continued talking.

"Bitch you think I wonna do this? Hell naw, but I want to be an actress and I know I can't do that unless I get the fuck out of Memphis and to get out I gotta get my cake up!" Benzi said pulling hundred dollar bills out of her bra top.

"I turn me off when I hit this club. When I come through that doe, I'm Benzi, "The Money Maker" that's it!" She said getting the blunt from Nika and taking a big, deep hit.

"Now bitch, turn yo feelings the fuck off and come on let's get this money!" Beniz said putting her money in the money bag around her wrist and hitting her blunt again.

"What you said?" Lakea said laughing as she stood up.

She knew exactly what Benzi was talking about. As long as she remembered her reason for stripping and knew who she truly was she would be fine. Just like in Wolverine she would have to tuck her true self away within and be whoever the situation called her to be. Right then she had to be seductive, sexy, provocative, and enticing.

'I can do all that and more.' She thought to herself.

"Let's do this", Lakea said smacking Benzi on her fat, tattooed ass making it jiggle.

"Oooh, that's how I like it. Now let's go money maker." Benzi said standing back and letting Lakea walk out of the dressing room first.

"I'm bout to be all over your fine ass on stage." Benzi said following Lakea out of the dressing room with her eyes on her ass.

As Lakea stood backstage and the music blasted through the speakers, she felt outside of herself. Like she was watching everything happen through someone else's eyes. It just didn't seem real to her. She watched Benzi adjust her g-string and tiny Chanel skirt, then looked back and smile at her.

"It's yo time bitch. Let's get this money!" Benzi said walking up the last two steps of the stage as the DJ's voice echoed through the speakers.

"Alright, alright all you ballers and broke niggas, coming to the stage, we got a real treat for you ugly muthafuckas. Two lovely ladies like no other, the veteran and the newbie, vanilla and caramel, the one and only Ms.

Benzi and the All-Star Newcomer KANDIIIIII!!!" The DJ yelled.

Lakea swallowed hard and closed her eyes, it was time to let Kandi perform.

Chapter 10

As the strobe lights came on Benzi stepped forward on to the stage with Lakea right behind her. Lakea's butterflies had totally disappeared as she walked on to the stage and straight up to a group of dudes standing in front of the stage with hundreds of dollars in their hands. Lakea walked slowly and seductively to the dudes, keeping her eyes on the obvious leader who was draped in diamonds and gold. When she was just out of arms reach, Lakea turned around and began to make her ass jump to the beat of the song, "I'm In Love with a Stripper". She twerked her ass cheeks and whipped her long hair from side-to-side just as Mesha had showed her. Lakea heard the guys start to yell and saw that they were throwing handfuls of dollars and five's, but she wanted the big money. She dropped to her knees and began to make her ass clap to the beat. More money was thrown, but still no twenties or hundreds. Lakea looked over to the side to see Benzi making her ass clap in some fat guy's face as his friends made it rain on her. That's what Lakea wanted.

She turned and crawled seductively up to the guy draped in diamonds, licking her lips and keeping eye contact. He stared at her intently as she began twerking her ass again, while looking at him. She unhooked her skirt letting it drop to the ground as she revealed her black, lace G-string and plump, naked, caramel ass. Lakea crawled to the edge of the stage and sat down, still staring at her guy. Then she opened her legs and began twerking her pussy in the guy's face. His friends erupted in cheers as they threw money at Lakea. The diamond guy kept his eyes on Lakea the whole time, gripping her ass and holding two stacks of money in his other hand that had to be at least $5,000 each stack. Lakea lie back on stage with her legs in the air making her ass shake as she unlaced the front of her corset. The guy with the diamonds stared at her like he was possessed, while fanning money off one of his stacks at her. Lakea saw $20's, $50's, and $100's. When she began to lick her own breast while rubbing her pussy through her lace panties the guys began to go frantic making it rain on her again. Benzi saw how well Lakea's group of guys was tipping so she danced her way to the side of the stage they were on. She immediately dropped to her knees, while twerking her ass, burying her face in Lakea's crotch. This made the guys go wild and they started throwing handfuls of money. Lakea didn't know how to feel, she was totally taken off guard. She knew that she and Benzi would have to touch at some point on stage, but she didn't expect it to go this far. She could feel Benzi's warm, wet tongue on her pussy lips and it made her feel weird because she wasn't a lesbian. However, it had been a long time since she had sex, and her second roll pill was just kicking in.

'Fuck it!' Lakea thought as she grabbed the back of Benzi's head moving it in a circular motion and licking her left breast again.

"This right here is a show!" The DJ yelled. "Y'all muthafuckas better get y'all cheap asses up and tip. All this ass on the stage and y'all sitting down!"

And the dudes did. They made it rain on Lakea and Benzi as they danced and worked the pole for two more songs. To Lakea's surprise she was a natural at the pole, which must have been a result of her martial arts training and gymnastics as a child. She had the dudes watching her every move as she twerked her ass in the air and twirled around the pole upside down. She really turned the club up when she climbed to the top of the pole and dropped down really fast into a split. That is when the guy in diamonds motioned for her to come over when she got off the pole. When Lakea got over there he grabbed her around the waist and stuck the rest of an entire stack of $20's, $50's, and a few $100's into the front of her corset.

"Baby you bad." is all he could say as him and his friends began to bounce and dance to the music as "Cold Wit It", Blast through the speakers.

Lakea and Benzi danced around the stage collecting their money as Lakea noticed the guy she cursed out outside the club sitting in the corner watching her. He gave her an eerie feeling, but she shrugged it off and kept picking up her money. By the time Mesha and Nika joined Lakea and Benzi on stage to help pick up the money they already had two buckets almost full. When they finished picking up all of the cash and left the stage the girls had three crown royal bags and three buckets filled with money. Lakea was happy despite the nagging feeling she had in her heart. She knew it was her guilt and also Jeremy telling her she shouldn't be doing the things she was, but she had to do whatever it took to provide for the boys. That meant ignoring that nagging feeling.

As all of the girls sat in the dressing room counting up the money made on stage, Lakea noticed that the tips of her fingers had turned blue. She thought maybe something was on the money, so she ignored it.

"Okay, we got $4,800 right here, that's $2,400 a piece not including what we made individually when we had them niggas hemmed up on both sides of the stage. Bitch we hit they ass up!" Benzi said as she gave Lakea five and they both laughed.

After assessing her $4850 total take for the night, Lakea decided she was done. She still couldn't shake that nagging and eerie feeling, her fingers were still blue after three washes, and now she was feeling extremely tired and nauseous, and she was getting a headache.

"Y'all ready to go?" Lakea asked Mesha and Nika as they sat at the counter eating rotel dip and chips that the house mama, Cutie brought.

"Okay June, we will be ready as soon as we finish eating. We banked anyway might as well go home." Mesha said smacking on her food.

"Why you not eating anyway. Hoe you getting all sick and shit. You preggo?" Nika asked laughing.

"Bitch hell no, by who? Anyways…" Lakea said rolling her eyes at Nika and licking her tongue out.

"Shut up hoe. I do feel kind of bad though and the smells in here ain't making it no better, so Ima go sit in the car and wait on y'all."

"Aite, be careful. Here take my purse, 'cause bitch you know I stay strapped," Mesha said taking her black Chanel purse with the pearl handle 9MM inside out of a locker and handing it to Lakea.

Lakea dressed quickly, got Benzi's cell phone number and then exited the club using the same door they came in. It was almost 4:00 a.m. when Lakea stepped out of the side door. The fresh, cool night air hit her in the face hard as soon as she stepped on the sidewalk.

"Aw hell naw beautiful.", a short, very handsome young guy working security named lil Mitch said as Lakea walked past him standing by the side door smoking a blunt. "I gotta make sure that you get to your car safely sexy. I wouldn't be a man if I didn't." Lakea smiled at lil Mitch as he passed her the blunt and continued to walk with her.

"We may as well smoke and walk, so you fina go? Where yo cousin nem at?" Lil Mitch asked.

"Oh, those heifas ain't ready to go yet. Ima wait in the truck though cause I think all them smells in the dressing room making me sick."

"Hell, it's some stanky muthafuckas in there, niggas and bitches so I ain't surprised you got sick!" Lil Mitch said laughing as Lakea passed him the blunt back.

Just as they reached the truck, they heard a lot of loud noises and voices coming from the right side of the parking lot.

"What the fuck going on over there?!" Lil Mitch yelled as he and Lakea walked closer to see a group of six guys standing near and open car door. "Maine what the fuck y'all doing?" Lil Mitch yelled again as the guys suddenly stopped talking and moved aside so that Lakea and lil Mitch could see.

There was a girl in dance clothes lying halfway on the ground and halfway in the car and her eyes were tightly shut, but her body was shaking, and she was foaming at the mouth.

"What the fuck happened and who the fuck is she?" Lil Mitch asked.

All the boys shrugged, indicating no one knew who she was or what happened to her. Lakea just stood there staring at the girl. She couldn't take her eyes off of her. She was staring at the girl the same way she had done when she was 14 living in LMG, and she saw that boy shot from her window. Death wasn't anything new to Lakea, but now that she was a mother, she valued life more. She felt sorry for the girl, she was someone's daughter.

"Take her to the hospital!" Lakea yelled at the dudes.

"We was trying to do that. That's why she in the car. Maine, we don't even know who this bitch is. She was selling pussy on the lot then she walked up asking for a light talking about she took three double stacks and was feeling good. Next thing a nigga know this bitch fell out and started shaking and foaming at the mouth", one of the dudes said as he lit his cigarette.

"Well get her junky ass the fuck off the lot." Lil Mitch said. "Take that hoe anywhere but here,"

"Hell naw." the driver of the car said as he and two more dudes got back into the car. "I ain't taking this bitch to no damn hospital so they can think I did something."

"Please take her!" Lakea yelled as the boy slammed his car door a sped out of the parking lot.

Lakea stood there still staring at the car as it sped down the street until Lil Mitch put his arm around her and start leading her to Mesha's truck.

"You can't feel sorry for every hoe that you meet lil mama." Lil Mitch said as he helped Lakea into the passenger seat of Mesha's truck. "That shit will drive you crazy. Around here it's fuck yo feelings. Well goodnight witcho sexy ass!" Lil Mitch said closing the truck door.

"Goodnight." Lakea said as she lay her head back on the seat and drifted off.

She wasn't sleep long because soon Mesha was banging on the truck window to get in. Lakea opened her eyes and unlocked the doors as she moaned because her headache was now a full-on migraine. She got out of the passenger seat and got in the back to stretch out across the seat. All she wanted to do was to get home and into her soft, warm bed. Lakea sunk into the backseat as Mesha started up the truck and bolted off the lot.

"You okay?" Nika asked Lakea, while reaching in the backseat and touching her shoulder.

"Girl I feel awful." Lakea said looking at her friend.

"It was probably those rolls and that liquor. You just need to go sleep it off." Nika said.

Just then the girls went under an overpass and Lakea caught a glimpse of a woman lying under the bridge and she had on the same clothes as the girl she had just saw passed out.

"She dead!" Lakea yelled so loud Mesha quickly stopped the car.

Lakea described to Nika and Mesha what she had saw earlier. Nika called the police on her cell phone and they waited until they heard the sirens approaching. At home Lakea still felt bad, not only was her body acting stupid and she had this nagging feeling in her heart, now she couldn't get the memory of the girl laying on the ground under the bridge out of her head. It was a sign that the lifestyle really wasn't for her, but like many times in the past she never followed the signs.

"We gone spend the night with you June." Mesha said walking into Lakea's room and sitting on the bed.

"I already called my mama and told her. The boys are fine. You need to go to sleep though cousin, you look bad,"

"I feel bad too." Lakea said weakly.

"Well goodnight." Mesha said as she got up and turned off the lights, exiting the room as she closed the door behind her.

Those were the last words that Lakea heard before she fell into a deep sleep.

The next morning Lakea woke up to excruciating pain all over her body. The pain in her body was so overwhelming it took her breath away. She tried to yell for Mesha or Nika to help, but she couldn't. Lakea decided to try to make it to the bathroom, but as soon as her feet hit the floor and she tried to take a step she got dizzy. The whole room started spinning and Lakea reached out trying to catch her balance on the wall. Instead, she fell into the nightstand causing her lamp to fall to the floor with a loud crash and shatter into a thousand pieces. The noise from Lakea's breaking lamp woke Mesha and Nika up out of a sound sleep and they both came running to Lakea's room.

"KEA!" was the last thing Lakea heard before everything went black and her limp body hit the floor.

Lakea woke up what seemed to be three months later, but it was only 45 minutes. However, when she tried to move, she was still in a great deal of pain and she felt dizzy. She was in the hospital once again with Mesha, Nika, Quan, and to her surprise, Ray-Ray at her side. Lakea didn't know it but her big brother Ray-Ray was never far away. He would always come by the house without her knowing it to check on them and get a glimpse of his boys. He wasn't so far gone on drugs and sorrow that he didn't care. He just didn't know how to deal with his grief.

"Ray-Ray! Hey big bruh!" Lakea said attempting a smile.

A tear ran down her face as her big brother took her hand in his and kissed it.

"You gone be okay lil sis, they really don't know what's wrong other than you're dehydrated, and they say you may have a stomach virus. They supposed to send you to a specialist soon." Ray-Ray said taking a seat next to Lakea. "You gotta take it easy though lil sis, and I'm gone help you. I signed up for rehab last week, I go in tomorrow. I'm gone get my shit together lil sis and help you again. Be the big brother I once was."

Those words made Lakea feel so much better in her spirit; however, her body was still in pain. Lakea had waited for the day to hear her brother say those words. There was nothing she wanted more than to have her big brother back. Lakea began to cry as Ray-Ray and Quan hugged her.

"Oohhh, I'm hurting." Lakea cried out as she lies back on her pillow.

"Push this button for morphine." Nika said pressing the button attached to the cord coming from Lakea's IV drip.

"Your ass tina be high as fuck in a second." Mesha said with a smile.

Suddenly Lakea felt a wave of calm rush over here. Finally, no more pain and she drifted off to sleep; dreaming about her life, from the outside like she was watching a movie. She saw all of the tragedy, all of the pain, the scared, hurt little girl she used to be and the broken young woman she now was. She saw all the bad times and the good times; her love for Jeremy and his love for her, her beautiful son, and her nephew. The dream played out just like a movie, except she couldn't see her future, only silhouettes of this happy family. Lakea woke up in a cold sweat hoping that was her happy family in the dream. Maybe in the future she wouldn't be broken.

Lakea was released from the hospital that evening, and she went home feeling better than she went in. However, she still had an aching pain all over her body and would get tired very easily. The pain and stiffness Lakea had in her joints caused her to start missing work at the cable company as each day was a struggle to get out of bed. It took her to noon each day to reduce her pain enough to go to the bathroom on her own. Felicia and Mesha were there a lot to help Lakea with day-to-day things, and to watch the boys. After about two weeks Lakea began to find a balance between the pain meds she was popping and Kush she was smoking that allowed her to go to work part-time at the Cable Company and weekends at the club. She had to pay the bills. However, in the process of self-medication, working, sorrow, and uncertainty, Lakea began to lose herself. Everything had become a blur between the drugs, the pain, the bills, dancing, her job, and a horrible past that always found a way to manifest itself in her current situation. That broken girl was trying to pick up the pieces of her shattered life, but she was going about it all wrong.

Ray-Ray came home from rehab after 30 days and he was even better than before. He was clean and dealing with his grief, and he had started back being a great father to his kids. Once out of rehab he had gotten a job as a garbage man driving the truck and was bringing in a stable income, helping Lakea with the bills. Things were okay for a change. Quan was leaving in a couple of weeks for school after a short delay and despite the occasional tiredness and the constant pain, Lakea was doing well. In her spirit she had a little peace. She was sleeping more, smiling more, and she even started back writing songs.

"It's time to change", Lakea said out loud as she sat on the porch with J-J in her arms and Ray-Ray pushed Ray-Jay and Rahiem on the swing set next to the porch.

"What you say?" Ray-Ray asked Lakea as he looked at her.

"Big bruh I'm 20 years old and I have nothing to show for it other than being a damn stripper." Lakea said in a somber tone, kissing her son on his head as he played with his Elmo doll. "I gotta stop this shit. We doing better now, so I'm done. If it wasn't Benzi's birthday, I wouldn't be going to the club tonight. I'm just gone make a quick appearance then I'm leaving. I'm tired of that shit!" Lakea said in a serious tone.

Ray-Ray smiled a huge smile. He was so proud of his sister. Although he never liked the fact that she was dancing he never told her so. He wanted her to make her own decisions. Now he was just happy she had come to the point in her life where she was ready to let go of the negative things and stop letting the past influence her decisions.

"Well, you know I'm behind you lil sis 100%. You can always depend on that.", Ray-Ray said walking over and hugging his sister. "Go out tonight and have fun, not work. I'm taking the boys to mama over Aunt Violet's house, and me and Quan going out. I'm coming back over her afterward though. I know you hate to be alone, witcho shaky ass." Ray-Ray said laughing and pushing his sister.

"But forreal, go have fun and say goodbye to that club forever and then come home and let's start our lives over. That type of shit ain't you anyway." Ray-Ray said.

"I know bruh, besides, I can feel something bad happening if I stay my ass in that club", Lakea said getting up and preparing to go into the house.

Lakea didn't know how right she was, but she would soon find out. As Lakea pulled up to the club that evening she had a feeling in her soul that something wasn't right.

"I'm just gone run in, give Benzi her gift, and be the fuck out." Lakea said to herself as she applied her lip gloss in the rear-view mirror.

"Alright, let's close this chapter." she said as she got out of the car and walked towards the front door of the club.

Just then she felt someone grab her arm and a male voice say, "Yeah wasup now baby. I got my bank up so I know I'm fucking tonight." the guy said as he slapped Lakea on the ass as hard as he could.

It was the dude from the first night Lakea had danced. The creepy nigga she had told to holler at her when he got his bank up. Seems he had done just that. Lakea's reflexes, training, and past trauma reacted before she could think, and she spun around fast delivering a hard chop right across the due's throat. The impact of the lick sent him flying backwards on to the ground holding his throat and gasping for air. The crowd of guys standing at the entrance watching it all go down laughed and yelled as Lil Mitch rushed Lakea into the club, and other security guards beat the creep's ass all the way to his car.

Lakea was irritated when she finally got into the club, so after giving Benzi her gift, having a few drinks and dancing off stage with her friends, Lakea was ready to go. Lil Mitch walked Lakea to her car at about midnight; she had only been in the club for an hour and a half. Driving home Lakea began to feel tired and the pain in her legs started up again. She also had an eerie feeling like she was being watched. That was the same feeling she had on stage the night she met the creep. Lakea quickly dismissed the thought that someone was watching her and just blamed her symptoms on the alcohol she had consumed. When Lakea pulled into her driveway she was so happy to be home. She was exhausted both mentally and physically.

The house was completely dark when Lakea got out of her truck and walked up the driveway. Lakea figured Ray-Ray and Quan were still out. She hoped that they would come home soon because she hated to be at home alone. She had been alone enough in her life. As Lakea walked to her door she heard a car door close somewhere a couple of houses down. Lakea didn't know why but the sound of that door slam made her feel scared. Her head suddenly began to throb, and she felt sick. Her hands shook as she put her key in the door and began to turn the knob. She couldn't' wait to get inside where she was safe and lay down. Just then the hair on the back of Lakea's neck stood up. Lakea slowly turned her head to see who was coming up behind her. Before she could think, or her eyes could even focus she was being tackled to the floor. Whoever pushed her was now on her back straddling her with his hand over her mouth. He kicked the door close and then delivered four punches to the back of Lakea's head and back. She moaned and yelled out in agony from the vicious blows. She was already in so much pain.

"Noo, please stop." Lakea pleaded as the guy turned her over so that she was facing him.

"Stop begging bitch. You was tough as a muthafucka when you was at the club talking shit and chopping niggas across the throat, now yo funky ass begging", The dude said.

Lakea's eyes widened as she stared up into her attacker's face. She recognized him instantly, it was the creep.

"It's you, please…" Lakea began but the creep cut her off.

"Yeah, bitch it's me!" he yelled as he began to punch Lakea in her face and choked her until she blacked out.

Check Out These and Other Hot Reads From The Desk of Best-Selling Author Niki Jilvontae…Available on Amazon!!!

1963

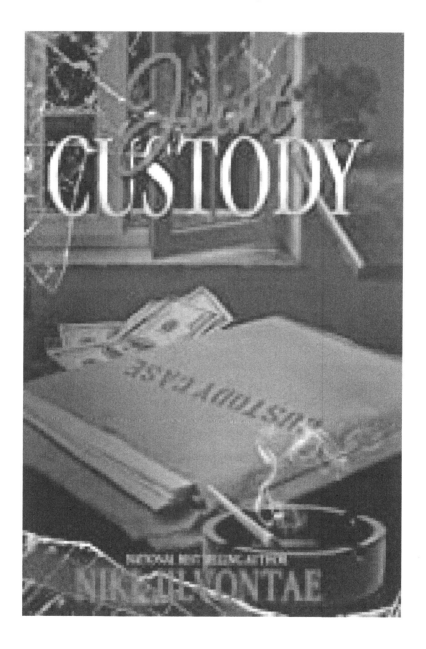

Made in the USA
Monee, IL
28 April 2021